Weekend Collision
A Crossing Forces HEA Story

Weekend
COLLISION

USA Today Bestselling Author
C.A. SZAREK

Weekend Collision
C.A. Szarek

A Crossing Forces HEA Story

Paper Dragon Publishing
North Richland Hills, TX

eBook ISBN: 978-1-941151-37-2
Paperback ISBN: 978-1-941151-38-9

Published in the United States of America

First eBook Edition: February, 2018
First Print Edition: February, 2018

Other Books by C.A. Szarek

Crossing Forces — Romantic Suspense

Collision Force (Book One) — *Coming soon to Audio!*
Cole in Her Stocking (A Crossing Forces Christmas) — *FREE read!*
Chance Collision (Book Two)
Calculated Collision (Book Three)
Collision Control (Book Four)
Weekend Collision (A Crossing Forces HEA Story) — *FREE read!*
Superior Collision (Book Five)
Incendiary Collision (Book Six) — *Coming soon!*

The King's Riders — Epic Fantasy Romance

Sword's Call (Book One) — *Also in Audio!*
Love's Call (Book Two) — *Also in Audio!*
Rogue's Call (Book Three) — *Also in Audio!*
Fate's Call (A Novella from the World of the King's Riders) — *Also in Audio!*

Highland Secrets — Historical Fantasy/Time Travel

The Tartan MP3 Player (Book One)
The Fae Ring (Book Two)
The Parchment Scroll (Book Three)
Highlander's Portrait (A Highland Secrets Story) — *Coming soon to Audio!*
Highland Valentine (A Highland Secrets Story) — *only .99*
The Princess and The Laird (A Highland Secrets Prequel)

Highland Treasures — Historical Fantasy/Time Travel

Highland Oath (Book One) — *Coming January 2018!*
Highland Essence (Book Two) — *Coming soon!*

Anthologies

Deep in the Hearts of Texas — *FREE read!*
   Story: Promise (A Crossing Forces Companion)

Chapter 1

THE TODDLER'S GIGGLE had Mel pausing in the doorway, her palm hovering over her lower stomach. Envy made her ache from the inside out.

Or is that just cramps?

She frowned and forced her feet into the living room.

Jared's deep chuckle had her grinning, despite the dark thoughts.

Her husband's long muscular form lay stretched out on their couch, his partner's two-year-old perched on his middle, as if he was the sofa. He didn't seem to mind as the little boy played with a large stuffed red airplane, waving it back and forth.

Shiny silver fabric sewn in the front *'windows'* caught the light of the lamp behind them. Micah made engine noises as he 'flew' the plane, tugging on the soft wings.

"Buddy, if people are on that plane, you're rattling their brains." Jared laughed.

"No!" Micah announced.

His mother had assured them the word was his new favorite.

Seeing her man with the child hurt in a way it never had before.

The toddler's dark hair curled at the ends, and could have him passing as Jared's kid, if it wasn't for Andi's eyes. Then again, Mel had blue eyes, too. Just lighter in hue.

Her husband was great with kids, especially Cole and Andi's little boys.

He'd make a great dad.

Someday…

Her chest burned and her heart skipped.

When they heard her, both males grinned up at her, and it was hard not to be sucked into Micah's big sapphire eyes.

Jared's smile faded as he gave her a onceover. "What's wrong, baby?"

Mel plastered on a return smile. "Nothing." She took her previous seat in the recliner facing the TV and pretended not to feel his gaze. Forced a breath and glanced at the man she loved.

Her husband's dark eyes reflected disbelief.

She never could lie to him and get away with it.

"Aunt Mel, look." Ethan, the elder of the two brothers, at six, scrambled off the floor, a tower of Legos in both hands. "I made a castle."

Saved by the kid, thank God.

"That's awesome!" She paid proper attention and inspected the multi-colored blocks, smiling and commenting until the little boy returned to the pile of scattered toys on the floor.

The *Minions Movie* played on the TV, but neither child seemed interested.

She sighed and slid back into the microfiber chair she loved. Then reached for her cup of hot cocoa on the end table and took a sip. Needed to drink it before it got cold.

The boys and Jared had already finished theirs.

Suddenly, the weight of Mel's trip to the bathroom crashed down on her shoulders and made her heart stutter.

She'd started her period.

Again.

She didn't want to tell Jared. Didn't want to see disappointment in the dark eyes she loved so much.

I'm still not pregnant.

They'd only been trying a few months, and she'd been on birth control for years, so it wasn't abnormal. Only natural it might take a while. There was nothing *wrong*. Rational, as well as medical answers floated in her head.

Dr. Hayes, her OBGYN, had told them how everything worked. Google and WebMD had verified.

Obsessed much?

Andi, the boys' mom, and a police detective like Jared and their dad, Cole, had told her she was worrying too much. Told her to take a breath, stop *trying* to try so hard.

Mel hadn't shared the extent of her worries with her husband, because she was embarrassed.

'*There's nothing* wrong *with you,*' Andi had told her just that afternoon when they'd dropped their sons off for a rare weekend away.

She was having a hard time believing it.

That was *before* she'd answered Mother Nature's knock.

Mel loved the boys; she really did. Loved kids, in general. They were her job, her life.

She'd had Ethan in her kindergarten class last year. Missed him this year, though she enjoyed her new students like always. She was lucky to still have Ethan in her life, although in a different capacity. She was *Aunt Mel*, not *Miss Nash*—Mrs. Manning—this year at school.

She and Jared had been married nine months now, and the school year had been going since the second week of August.

Thanksgiving was just around the corner—in two weeks.

They were supposed to have waited until the previous June to marry, but after getting engaged Christmas Day, they'd impulsively flown to Vegas when the wedding planning had become too stressful.

Valentine's Day weekend—when everybody and their brother had had the same idea.

Couples had been lined up in all the chapels.

When it'd been their turn, Mel hadn't seen anyone but Jared.

"Hey."

His voice pulled her from memories and her eyes locked onto his.

"Talk to me, baby. What's wrong?"

She gestured to their weekend charges. "Nothing." She swallowed and made her smile wider. "I'll talk to you later."

"Do I need to be worried?"

She shook her head. "Nope."

Jared nodded, but his expression called her a liar.

The credits started to roll on their large flat-screen, farewell music accompanying the scrolling words.

"Uncle Jared, can we watch another movie? I want more minions!" Ethan's red curls shifted as he cocked his head to one side.

"Sure, dude. Anything for you."

Mel got up and ejected the Blu-Ray from their player.

"I can do it myself!" The little boy jumped to his feet and carefully pulled the disc out, then handed it to her.

She thanked him and gave him the second movie, which'd been sitting on top of the player. "Do you want to put it in?"

"Yes! I can do it!"

She supervised, then returned to her seat as the previews for Pixar's upcoming stories started to play. "Good job, Ethan!"

He grinned, flashing the gap of his missing teeth. That afternoon, he'd proudly announced he'd received a twenty dollar bill under his pillow just that morning for losing the pair.

Cole had grumbled something about the tooth fairy being tired, but Andi had elbowed his arm when he'd offered to hold onto the money for his son.

She'd told him it was a natural consequence of not paying attention—half-asleep or not—and they'd all laughed.

Mel laughed again.

"Something funny?" Jared asked, one corner of his mouth lifting.

"Just remembering the tooth fairy's *mistake*."

Her husband chuckled. "Right. Cole meant to give him a fiver."

"Shhh, he'll hear you." However, one glance at the child told her Ethan had abandoned the Legos on the floor and was glued to the movie.

Micah buzzed his stuffed plane and crashed it into her husband's chest.

"Ohhhh, owwwww."

The toddler fell into a fit of giggles as Jared clutched his supposed injury with both hands.

Mel shook her head, but she couldn't stop watching them together. Sadness and fear washed over her.

What if that would *never* be them?

Her eyes swept the living room. Toys the boys had brought were strewn all over, and it brought a smile to her lips. One afternoon was all it had taken for Ethan and Micah to hijack their place.

It looked…natural.

Their things…belonged.

She swallowed. Blinked to clear her vision and looked away from her husband so he couldn't catch on.

Mel wanted Jared's baby in her belly, then in her arms. So they could play, like he was with his partner's son on his lap.

Chapter Two

EVENING FADED INTO night, and Mel read to Ethan as Jared put the baby to bed after a bath. They fell into a normal rhythm as if they had the boys all the time.

He didn't like the look on her face when he joined her in their bedroom.

Something is *wrong.*

She sat on the end of their bed, freshly showered and dressed for bed in a feminine pink tank top and matching boxers. She combed her light brown waves out so they wouldn't tangle.

"Why didn't you wait for me?" Jared stuck his lip out, trying to get a smile.

They often showered together. He wished she would've waited so he could've held her, or at least coaxed her to tell him what was up.

He wouldn't have had to keep his hands to himself either way.

His stomach dipped when Mel didn't even look at him.

"Sorry, with the boys here, I thought it'd be better." She shrugged.

"They're two and six. Like they'd know the difference. Besides, they're both fast asleep." Jared sighed when she still didn't spare him a glance.

She didn't say anything, so he closed the door and crossed the room.

"I told Ethan to come right in if he needed us. Micah curled up right next to big brother on the bed. Cole said they've been doing the toddler bed thing for a few months, so I'm not so worried he'll roll off and get hurt."

"Yeah, they'll be fine. Ethan has that ridiculously huge bear they both love. They'll sleep well." Mel finally looked at him. A soft smile curved her delectable mouth, but it looked sad.

"Hope so." He waggled his eyebrows and tugged his gray tee over his head.

"I started today," she blurted.

Oh.

Jared tossed the shirt into a basket and knelt in front of his wife. Pulled the comb from her limp fingers and put it on the bed. He took both her hands, spreading kisses all over her knuckles. "That's what you're upset about?" His heart skipped when she nodded. Her beautiful crystal blue eyes misted over.

"I'm sorry." Her whisper was wobbly.

"What the heck for?" He pushed off the floor and sat next to her on their king sized bed. Made her look at him.

She swallowed.

He wanted to kiss her throat.

She lowered her lashes. "I…"

"Mel."

His wife turned her face away, but not far enough he didn't notice how she sucked in her bottom lip.

"Mel. Look at me."

A tear rolled down when she obeyed.

Jared cupped her cheek and thumbed it away. "I love you," he whispered.

"I love you, too." Her words shook, so he drew her into his arms and sighed.

He never felt more like a stupid guy than at moments like these. Didn't have a clue what to say. He wanted kids, yeah. But he wasn't stressed about it.

It'd happen for them when it was supposed to. He sure as hell didn't mind the attempts. Would rather *not* keep his hands to himself where Mel was concerned.

Jared pressed a kiss to her temple and squeezed her tight when she burrowed into his chest.

"I don't know what's wrong with me."

Her statement was muffled against his skin, but her warm breath sent a tingle down his spine.

"Nothing is *wrong* with you, Melody Renee Manning." He shook her lightly and she looked up at him.

She sighed. "I don't mean physically. I mean emotionally. I'm a wreck for no reason."

"Well, it *is* that time—"

Mel smacked his chest. "Don't you *dare*."

He smirked. "*You* said it."

She narrowed her eyes and mock-glared. "Do you want to sleep on the couch, Detective Manning?"

He chuckled. "Don't do that to me when the boys are here. Ethan'll tell Cole and then there'll be questions about arguments in front of the children."

A smile played at her lips and Jared couldn't help it.

He dipped down and claimed her mouth. Told himself not to get lost to her, but he did, like always.

Conscious thought faded as their tongues danced, and someone moaned. His cock jumped in his jeans, letting his zipper take a bite.

Mel finally pulled away, but they both panted. "I can't…"

"I know, baby." He cupped her face and ran his thumbs back and forth over her cheekbones. Her beauty stunned him, like always. Especially with her lips kiss-swollen and flushed pink.

"I feel like a failure." Her pretty eyes watered, making the hue shine.

Even that was beautiful, although he hated when she cried.

"You're *not* a failure. These things take time. You know how long it took Nikki and Pete. Yet, they have little Brenna now."

She nodded in his grip, then grabbed his wrist and squeezed. "I'm still sorry."

"Then you're silly. We'll have kids, Mel. Even if we have to buy one."

She laughed and tugged away gently. "That might be a little illegal."

"Happens all the time."

His wife smirked. "I thought you already skirted the law one time too many, Detective."

"Don't remind me." Jared's mirth faded a bit when he thought about his older brother in prison, even though Joe had turned himself in.

Prison was still better than getting killed by the bastard that was still on the run.

"Sorry, I don't want to upset you…"

He shook his head. "No worries. Listen. I love you. That's all that matters. And next week, when you're done, we can practice making babies again."

Mel grinned and his stomach fluttered. "Promise?"

"Like I could keep my hands off you."

She laughed and Jared kissed her again.

"Let's go to bed, there are two little boys here that don't really sleep *in* much," she whispered against his lips.

"Right. Especially with a promise like a trip to the zoo."

She groaned. "It's going to be a long day."

"Yeah, but fun."

"Hey, Ethan can spend the tired tooth fairy's gift."

He chuckled. "That he can."

"Thanks for making me feel better." Mel smiled softly.

"Anytime, baby. Anytime." He kissed her one last time before ditching his jeans and crawling into bed.

Chapter Three

MICAH *OOOHHED* AND *awwwed* when Jared hiked him higher in his arms.

Ethan stood beside them, his face practically plastered to the glass outside the white tigers' enclosure, trying to get a better view of the two cubs rolling around batting at huge hanging knotted ropes.

Mel stood behind them, manning the massive stroller Andi had left for them to use. It was handy for storing all the toddler and little boy paraphernalia, but it was a pain to lug around.

With the seat empty, no less, because their two-year-old charge preferred to be held or walk on his own. Whined when his bidding was disregarded.

"No!" and "I can do it!" had become the mantra for the morning, and well into the afternoon.

She swallowed back a yawn. They'd left at seven-thirty to make the drive in to Fort Worth, and despite nestling in her husband's arms all night, she hadn't slept much.

"Your family is beautiful."

The voice had her head turning, and her gaze rested on an older woman watching Jared and the boys instead of the big cats.

"It's always nice to see an involved father." The pleasantly plump woman wore an outfit that screamed *Golden Girls*. Her hair was groomed in typical Texas big style and her smile was sweet.

Mel didn't feel like explaining, so she flashed a return smile and thanked her. Plus, her gut ached a little. It would be a long time before she and Jared could take their own children to the zoo. If they ever had any.

Her husband waggled his eyebrows over his shoulder. Evidently he hadn't been so absorbed with the tigers or the boys.

"So handsome, too. Lucky lady." The older woman reached out and patted Mel's hand, which rested on the stroller handle.

Jared grinned.

She wanted to roll her eyes—like her man needed help with his ego—but she just agreed politely. Was relieved when an older gentleman collected her. He wore a cowboy hat and boots and offered a nod.

"Okay, guys, let's go see the elephants," Jared said. He put Micah in the stroller, and for once the little boy didn't protest.

"Yay!" Ethan jumped up and down, then slid one of his hand in Mel's.

Micah rubbed his small fist against his eye and relaxed into his seat.

"Uh oh, someone's tired." Her husband dropped his voice and made eye contact with her.

"Thank God," she whispered.

"Am not," Micah announced. The high pitched toddler tones mixed with such vehemence made her smile again.

"How did he even hear me?" Jared chuckled.

"C'mon, Aunt Mel!" Ethan tugged her hand.

"Whoa, take a breather, buddy. Aren't you tired?" her husband asked.

He shook his head, his auburn curls floating.

"Of course not," Mel said.

"No more sugar!" Jared waggled his finger in Ethan's face, and the little boy giggled.

"I like cotton candy."

"Too much," she said.

"Are you having fun, Aunt Mel?" Ethan cocked his head to one side as he studied her.

"Yes, sir. Now, let's go. We have some elephants to see."

He jogged ahead as they started to move, but they let him, since he wasn't far.

Jared admonished him to stay close. Then sidled up and kissed her cheek.

Mel leaned into him and sighed. "Thanks," she whispered.

"You okay, baby? You've been awfully quiet today." He slid his arm around her as they walked.

"I am. Glad the boys are having fun."

"Hmm, but what about you? You didn't just lie to a child, did you?"

"You or Ethan?" She laughed at her husband's mock-glare.

"Well, at least I made you laugh, even at my own expense."

"That's usually the best kind." She winked.

"Hey!" He clutched his black T-shirt over his heart, but the grin he flashed made her melt a little.

Mel felt a little guilty for her desire to go home as the day wound on, but when they finally called it a late-afternoon, they had two tuckered out little charges.

Micah fell asleep before his car seat was buckled, and even Ethan was yawning as she helped him in to his booster.

The little boy flashed a sleepy smile as she reminded him to buckle up. Like his little brother, the first-grader liked to do things himself, and he could handle the fasteners on his booster.

"Did you have fun, buddy?" she asked.

"Yup!" He clutched a stuffed zebra close that Jared had bought. Ethan had saved his tired tooth fairy money at her husband's urging.

Micah's giraffe lay on his lap, tucked in one small hand, even as he slept.

She straightened, then shut the back door to her Kia SUV.

Jared was at the back of the car. He'd already unloaded the stroller, and was folding it like a pro.

"Need help?" she asked.

"Nope." He threw a smile at her as he made the last fold and lifted the behemoth thing into the back of the SUV. "Today was great." He closed the hatch.

Mel nodded.

"We can totally handle this parenting thing."

"They sure wear ya out, though," she said.

"Says the kindergarten teacher."

"That's different."

"Yeah?" He chuckled and pulled her to him. Jared brushed his mouth over hers.

She kissed him back, but pulled away before she got lost in him. They had the boys, after all.

He caressed her cheek, then glanced at his watch. "It's almost six. Wanna grab something to go instead of hitting a restaurant? They're both tired. With Micah that means grouchy and whiny."

"Same goes for Jared, too." She smirked.

"Hey!" He slapped her bottom and she yelped. Her husband beamed. He kissed her hard and fast. "So, let's get home, get them bathed and in bed. Watch a movie maybe?"

"Sure. As long as there are no more minions."

Jared laughed. "I meant a grown-up movie after the boys go to sleep."

"You're on." Mel grinned. She got in the car, glancing at the boys as she reached to snap her seatbelt on.

Ethan had fallen asleep, just like the toddler.

She and her husband exchanged another smile. "Thanks for today," she whispered, feeling much lighter than she had last night.

He arched an eyebrow as if to say, *'what for?'* but his dark eyes shone with understanding and love.

She relaxed into her seat.

Maybe her husband would have three sleeping passengers before they got home.

Chapter Four

THE *CRASH* MADE her wince. Mel had to consciously loosen her grip on the loaf of bread so she wouldn't smash it. Her gut told her the ruckus a few aisles over was nothing other than her husband and the two little boys still in their care.

Andi and Cole wouldn't be back until late Sunday afternoon, and now it was barely eleven.

Her sneakers screeched as she changed direction to leave the baked goods aisle and hurry—but not run—toward the raised voices.

She cringed when she heard Micah's familiar cry. "Jared?" she called even before she could see them. Had to dodge rolling cans of green beans.

Her husband was righting a grocery cart from its side on floor.

The store manager was fussing over them, a clipboard in hand. His balding hair got mussed as he bent over to pick up a bag of lettuce and tossed in it in the cart.

Tears streaked Ethan's cheeks, and Micah sat on the floor, his wail at glass-breaking pitch, and snot running down his face.

"I'm so sorry," Jared was telling the manager. And ignoring the kids.

"What happened?" Mel asked Ethan.

The little boy shook his head and looked at her husband. His chest rose and fell as he sniffled. His jeans were ripped over his right knee.

Concerned shoppers picked up cans of green beans, and an employee started restacking them.

If her memory served, they'd been in the shape of a huge pyramid before disaster—three names came to mind—had struck. Of course, only *one* person was really responsible.

Jared should've known better.

Mel dug in her purse for some tissues, then changed her mind and grabbed the baby wipes from the diaper bag. She squatted down in front of the crying two-year-old and wiped Micah's face.

He fought her at first, pushing her hands away, but she soothed him with whispered nonsense until tears were dry and snot was gone.

For now.

She stood and hiked him up on a hip, trying not to glare at the big tough police detective she'd married.

He was currently backpedaling as he explained the scene before them to the store manager. There was a lot of "Um..." as well as, "It was an accident."

Mel rolled her eyes and put the scenario together in her head. She never should've said, *"I'll be right back,"* and left them to get the bread.

Jared had had Micah in the cart and Ethan riding on the back—against her admonition in the first place.

He'd probably tried to make shopping *'fun.'* Maybe rushed down an empty aisle.

Ethan had probably jumped off the cart—or *onto* it—and tragedy had struck.

Her husband's version to the man taking notes was tame.

Mansplaining if I ever heard it.

She didn't believe a word.

"I'm sorry about the mess." At least he had the decency to look embarrassed. Jared's cheeks were a little pink, actually.

Good.

"Micah, does anything hurt?" She focused on the little boy in her arms. "Do you have a boo boo?"

He shook his head and sniffled, his big blue eyes shiny and his dark hair disheveled. He sucked his bottom lip into his mouth. His little chest heaved with residual sobs.

Mel looked at each of his hands, but there were no marks. His arms were okay, too. She tugged his red tee straight. No rip in his pants, like his older brother.

"Aunt Mel, my knee hurts." Ethan's voice grabbed her attention.

She set Micah to his feet so she could inspect the damage.

Blood trickled from a skinned knee, visible through the small hole.

"It's not too bad." She looked into the six-year-old's blue eyes and offered a reassuring smile. Caressed his cheek, wiping tears away. "We'll get you fixed up." She cleaned the small cut with a baby wipe, and grabbed a Band-Aid from the diaper bag. Andi really was prepared for everything. "What happened, buddy?" she repeated.

Ethan whimpered once, but thanked her. He looked at Jared before answering. "The cart fell over."

"Oh yeah? How?"

"We..." he sniffled again, fighting more tears, "went...too fast." He bit his bottom lip like his little brother.

"Don't worry, you're not in trouble. Your Uncle Jared is, I suspect."

Her husband glanced away from the store manager, as if he'd heard his name, and offered a half-smile. He ran his hand through his dark hair, like he always did when he was nervous.

Mel glared.

He winced, then turned back to the older man.

The groceries they'd had in the cart were scattered on the floor — including a carton of eggs lying open on its side. Shells and sticky yellow broken eggs covered the linoleum. The milk carton lay upside down, but it was holding its contents.

Canned goods rolled back and forth — not just the fallen tower of Green Giant. A box of Hamburger Helper was smashed, as well as the cereal.

She sighed and ruffled her former student's red curls, then got to down to the business of picking up the food on the floor.

Jared was still working his way through the incident report with the store manager.

Maybe she didn't need a kid. She already had one.

He just happened to be twenty-nine.

It was going to be a *looooong* morning.

"Just a hunch, but I figure Andi and Cole want their children back in the same condition they dropped them off in." Mel arched an eyebrow.

Jared shifted on his feet, feeling about two inches tall. "I'm sorry." He fought the urge to study his cowboy boots. "I'm sorry," tumbled out of his mouth again. It already had about hundred times.

I'm an idiot.

He'd said that, too, but didn't offer a repeat now, because he didn't want her to *agree* with him. He'd apologized to the store manager, all the employees, the boys, *and* Mel.

Thank God the only injury was a small scratch on Ethan's knee.

They'd paid for the damaged food anyway, but it was the least he could do for the freaking embarrassment.

He hadn't volunteered he was a cop, but Antioch wasn't that big. If the, *"let's have a little fun,"* blunder made its way to the PD, he'd *never* hear the end of it. Hopefully, none of the interior cameras had caught it.

Wouldn't that be some shit?

His partner was probably going to kick his ass for endangering his kids. Or, Cole would laugh his ass off. One never knew.

Mel snorted and put Micah in his car seat without answering.

I'm screwed.

His wife wouldn't argue in front of the kids, but after their parents picked them up, he was in for it. He should probably volunteer to sleep on the couch now and get it over with.

Ethan tugged his hand free of Jared's much larger grip.

He smiled down at the little boy. "Are you okay, E-man?"

Red curls bobbed. "Yup. Aunt Mel fixed my knee. It only hurts a little."

"Good deal. Put your seatbelt on, when you get in your booster, okay?"

The kid scrambled to obey.

Mel ruffled Ethan's hair and smiled when they passed each other, but the curve of her gorgeous mouth faded when she glanced at Jared. She narrowed her eyes and went around the front of her SUV. Wrenched the passenger door open and climbed inside.

He knew better than to say anything regarding her not helping with the grocery bags. Didn't want to pull couch duty for a *whole* week.

Scratch that.

She was furious. He was probably looking at two weeks.

A month?

Dammit.

Maybe he could cajole her. Use his charm. After all, they couldn't make a baby if they didn't sleep together.

Jared winced.

Her expression had said it all.

He wasn't getting laid for a while.

Jared put the bags in the back quietly and efficiently, inwardly cursing the fact it hadn't taken longer. He didn't want to slide into the driver's seat.

Hated when Mel was mad at him. This time was all his fault. *And* his best friend's kids could've gotten truly hurt.

He was torn between cowardice and shame.

Shit.

Dragging his hand through his hair, Jared swallowed a sigh and reached for the door handle. He'd take his medicine. Would have some explaining to do to his partner later, too.

Two sets of big blue eyes caught his line of sight in the rear-view mirror.

The boys were fine.

Score one for me.

A glance at Mel gifted another glare.

"I love you," he whispered.

She stared, then shook her head. "Don't do that when I'm trying to be mad at you." Her voice was low and she shot a glimpse over her shoulder at the kids.

"I hate when you're mad at me," Jared muttered.

"You deserve it. They could've been hurt. Really hurt."

"I know." He started the car and tried not to grimace. "I love them. I'd never want anything bad to happen to them."

"So irresponsible."

"*Now* you sound like a teacher."

Mel arched a fair eyebrow. "This is serious."

"I know, I know. I'm sorry."

She tossed her head into the headrest. "You're totally on your own with Cole and Andi."

"They're fine!"

"So? Still *your* mess, you clean it up."

"I will."

"If Cole clocks you, I won't say a word."

Jared snickered. "I bet he'll laugh."

She rolled her eyes. "Figures."

He smiled, and turned down Main Street, to head home. "No worries, baby. I got this."

"That's what I'm afraid of, I think."

He reached to pat her jean-clad thigh.

She squeezed his hand, which had him smiling all over again. Maybe Mel wasn't so mad at him after all.

"Just don't be reckless with other peoples' kids, okay?"

"You got it. What about our own?"

She smirked and his heart jumped, like always when she looked at him like that. "*I'd* kick your butt."

Jared chuckled and shook his head.

Chapter Five

MICAH THRE HIS arms around his mother's neck and kissed her with an enthusiastic *smack*.

Mel couldn't help the envy in her gut, either. Or the guilt that circled because of it. The feeling wasn't for Micah specifically. She had a special relationship with the little boy, even if he'd never call her '*Mommy.*' Didn't want Micah Lucas to call her that, anyway.

She just wanted what Andi had. The child. The bond. The little person who looked just like his dad.

"What's wrong, Mel?" Her friend's blue eyes were concerned as she set her two-year-old to his feet.

Mel swallowed a sigh. "Nothin'. Had a great weekend with the boys, notwithstanding '*the incident*' at Marty's."

Jared groaned at her air quotes and she flashed a smartass grin.

She'd meant it when she'd promised he'd be on his own regarding the toppled cart.

Cole arched a dark eyebrow.

Andi looked at Mel, Jared and back. Then at her husband. Her expression feared the worst.

"Of course, I'll let Jer tell you *all* about that." Mel beamed when her husband narrowed those beautiful mocha eyes she loved so much.

"The zoo was fun, Daddy!" Ethan announced, bouncing up and down and tugging on Cole's hand. "Uncle Jared bought me a zebra, and Micah got a giraffe!"

"That's awesome, E-man!" The tall detective ruffled red curls, then his steel gaze landed on his partner of three years. "What happened at the grocery store? Need I go request video footage?"

"Oh, God no." Jared pinned Mel with a glare. "Just remember, when they leave, you'll be stuck here. Alone. With me."

She giggled.

"Let's have a seat and you can tell me all about it." Cole's statement wasn't a suggestion.

"Don't kill him, okay? Sometimes I'm fond of him. But a maiming might be okay," Mel offered.

Her husband's partner wore an even more curious look, and threw his arm around Jared's shoulders.

When her man feigned right to get away from him, Cole smirked and playfully shoved him forward, sending the kids into a fit of giggles.

The guys faded into the living room, taking the boys with them. Deep voices mixed with Ethan's much higher one faded in and out.

Cole's laughter followed.

"Aren't you concerned?" Mel asked Andi, who'd stayed with her in the dining room.

"Nah, the boys are fine. Body parts all accounted for, no casts or limps." She winked, and took a seat at the table.

Mel grinned.

"I trust you guys, wouldn't leave my kids with you otherwise."

"I know. Appreciate that. We really did have a great weekend." She took a seat opposite her friend and sucked back another sigh.

The thousandth one of the weekend.

The female cop's gaze was already appraising.

Darn detective.

"Did you and Cole have a nice weekend? I bet it was great to get away."

Andi's pretty face lit up and her chestnut ponytail bobbed with her nod. "It was awesome. The bed and breakfast was really nice, and the couple that runs it convinced me romance never dies. They've been married forty years, and are so cute. Still so in love." She touched her cheek, and Mel smiled.

Her friend had no worries. Cole was completely head over heels for Andi. It was so obvious when they were together. But the detective hadn't been digging for affirmation. Her expression was wistful; she was no doubt reminiscing over the weekend.

"I think Cole missed the kids more than I did. But I kept him…distracted." She looked at Mel and flashed a grin that had them both laughing. Her face went pink up to her ears, contradicting her confession.

"That's great to hear."

"I love being a mom as much as I love being a cop, but sometimes parents need Mommy and Daddy time."

She shoved away the sadness that hit at Andi's lighthearted comment. She'd meant no harm. Mel swallowed and forced her eyes forward, instead of looking away like she wanted to.

Andi grabbed her hand. "Hey. What's up? For real."

"I hate that you notice stuff like that."

Her smile was unapologetic. "Pete would be proud; he's usually the more perceptive one."

She spoke of her partner; Mel had always liked the other detective, and his wife, Nikki.

"Nothing's wrong, really."

Her friend gave her a long look that called her a liar. After all, they'd talked about this before.

She sighed. "I started my period Friday night. No baby. Again. It's been months. Every time a start my period, I'm sure it's never going to happen. Jared says I need to be patient; that it'll happen when it's supposed to, but…" She blinked away sudden tears and broke eye contact.

"He's right, sweetie. Just relax. It *will* happen. Enjoy being with your man. Trying is fun. But we don't want to tell our husbands they're right, of course." Andi squeezed the hand she still held.

She forced another nod.

"Wow, no smile for me? Not even a little one? I was trying to be funny." Her eyes were wide when Mel looked back.

She managed a smirk. "I always enjoy being with Jared."

"Good."

"Babe, we should probably go. Gotta pack the car." Cole popped his head in the dining room and paused. "Oh, sorry, didn't mean to interrupt."

Mel stood. Made her lips curve up. "You didn't. Just chatting."

Andi rose and tugged her into a hug. "It'll be okay. Call me later if you wanna talk." She pressed a kiss to Mel's cheek. "Thanks again for keeping the boys. We had a great weekend."

"Anytime. I mean it. Your kids are awesome."

Cole flashed dimples and opened his arms. "Thanks. Ethan's going on about the fun he had. Probably will for days."

Mel went to her husband's partner and stepped into his hug.

"Get your hands off my wife," Jared playfully barked.

Cole held her tighter and she laughed. "Maybe I'll keep them both."

"Nah, two women are more trouble than one." Andi's voice was dry, but she grinned.

"Ain't that the truth," Cole quipped, and earned a smack from his wife.

They all laughed.

The guys shook hands and Mel kissed the boys.

Jared helped Cole get the boys' paraphernalia into Andi's SUV.

She waved as they pulled away, and couldn't help but sigh. Sat on the top step of their small porch.

The sun would set soon, and there was a great view from the front of their house.

"What's wrong, baby?" Jared drew her close when he took a seat beside her. His lips brushed her temple, then her cheek.

Instead of answering, she turned her face and met his mouth with hers.

It didn't take him more than half a second to deepen the kiss. Their tongues danced and dueled, and Mel wound her arms around his neck, nestling close.

He kissed her until her toes curled, and desire settled low in her belly, making her wish her period was already over.

Jared rubbed her back and held her afterward, her cheek resting over his heart.

She closed her eyes, savoring the comfort of the *thump thump* of his heart, she could feel as well as hear.

"You didn't answer me," he whispered, pressing another kiss to her temple.

"Nothing's wrong. Had a great weekend and I love sitting here like this with you."

"I love sitting here like this with you, too. Even if my ass is already going numb."

Mel laughed and lifted her head. "Don't ruin it."

He flashed a grin that had her insides wobbling. "Sorry."

"You aren't even." She poked his chest, and Jared chuckled.

"Probably not. I am grateful you're talking to me after '*the incident.*'" He made air quotes like she had earlier, and waggled his eyebrows.

She laughed again. "Well, you *are* lucky for that, I guess. What did Cole say?"

"He laughed, I told ya he would."

She rolled her eyes. "Men."

Jared's grin widened and his pressed his lips to her forehead. "On a serious note, he was grateful no one was hurt badly. Ethan piped up his knee had a boo boo, but Cole didn't kill me. If one of the boys would've been really hurt, I'm sure he would've."

"I would've arranged a nice funeral."

"Hey! That's all I mean to you?"

She grinned and cocked her head to one side. "Maybe."

Jared growled and kissed her.

Chapter Six

"I THOUGHT YOUR dad would never leave! At least my parents took a hint."

Mel glanced over her shoulder from the kitchen sink, trying to keep a straight face. "Wow, I'll be sure to let Daddy know how you really feel about him."

Hosting Thanksgiving, with their parents at their house for the first time had been fantastic, but her dad had stayed a few hours past pumpkin pie.

Her monitor told her she was ovulating, and she'd made the mistake of telling her husband that morning; Jared had been keyed up all day.

The touches and kisses he'd snuck for the majority of the day while they'd had company hadn't done much for keeping *her* libido in check.

Pushing him away never worked; her heart wasn't in it. Desire to sneak to the bedroom had been higher than spending time with her dad and his parents—as much as she loved them.

Sure, a little guilt assaulted her senses, but it was for a good cause—their first grandbaby.

Against her *real* wishes, Mel had told Jared to stop acting like a horny teenager, but he'd only flashed a wicked grin and kissed her again.

Her dad in the living room was too close for comfort, grown, married woman or not; need or not. Talked her out of whatever courage her hormones had mustered for sure.

Jared's hands swallowed her waist, and his warm breath tickled the back of her neck. His powerful chest cradled her back, and his erection through his jeans rubbed against her bottom.

Then his lips were nibbling, licking, kissing her neck and earlobe until her legs wobbled and she splashed warm, soapy water when her hands missed the first grab for the edge of the sink.

"Jared." His name came out more moan than protest, and she whirled in his arms, meeting his mouth when he dipped down.

He deepened the kiss, and rocked his hips in time with his tongue.

Her side hit the counter, but she didn't care.

Mel was a goner.

She couldn't tell him she needed to finish scrubbing a pan and put the leftover food away. Didn't care if it all rotted—she was liquid, grateful her husband was holding her up.

"I've been waiting to do that. All. Damn. Day." He panted against her, pushing the words into her lips, and his eyes were black with desire.

She could barely moan, let alone form a coherent thought.

Jared groaned and sealed his mouth over hers again, kissing her until her toes curled. He tore away on a ragged breath, and Mel's head spun. "Let's go to bed."

"Happy Thanksgiving," she whispered.

He grinned. "Baby, I'm thankful for you for damn sure."

Her heart skipped, which only made her dizzier. "I love you."

"I love you, too. And because I love you, I know you'll be mad at me if I whisk you away with a dirty kitchen, so I'll help you finish cleaning up."

Mel arched an eyebrow. "I feel like you have nefarious intentions."

Jared chuckled. "I *did* think about taking you on the butcher's block. But it's…busy."

She giggled and followed his gaze. The remnants of the turkey sat on her best platter at the center, but he'd already cut all the rest of the meat off it for her. "I do prefer our bed, truth be told."

His mouth hovered over hers, but he didn't kiss her properly. "Nah, sometimes you're adventurous."

That was true. They'd made love all over the house that'd been *hers*, but slipped to *theirs* effortlessly.

Tremors chased each other down her spine and she tipped up, begging without words.

Her husband retreated, instead of capturing her mouth again. "Let's get this done so I can ravish you without guilt."

Mel snorted. "Right. You'd be so bothered."

He winked and started putting the remainder of their meal away.

She stood back watching him, her heart thumping all over again.

Mel slipped her light blue sweater over her head, releasing it to the kitchen floor. Her bra was next, and she dropped it at her feet, then stepped out of her slippers. She'd given up real shoes after dinner.

Jared didn't notice she was getting undressed; he was diligently putting leftovers in containers and loading the dishwasher.

She grinned and shimmied out of her gray pencil skirt and pink panties, then perched her hand on her hip and waited for her man to notice she was naked in their kitchen.

He whirled toward the fridge, containers of mashed potatoes, stuffing, and green beans stacked in hands. His eyes widened and he froze a few inches from the handle. "Ummm…" His mouth hung open.

She laughed. "Wow. You'd think I did something wrong."

Jared recovered fast, sliding the food into the refrigerator, shutting it, and invading her personal space in what felt like the same move. "Not at all. Just surprised me, is all. Melody Manning is not a woman to be trifled with. Especially where her kitchen is concerned."

Mel laughed and wound her arms around his neck, moving in to his body heat. "I'm glad you recognize that."

His lips came down, but she met him, snuggling closer and kissing him back until she couldn't breathe.

"Butcher's block?" her husband asked against her mouth.

She smacked his chest and laughed again. "Bed."

"As you wish, my lady love."

She giggled, then yelped as he swung her up into his arms. Made a grab for his neck, but Jared wouldn't drop her.

Mel didn't speak — couldn't, since he fit his mouth over hers again, taking her air and her breath as he kissed her, but she didn't care if her head spun. Not when he was already sending her to heaven.

Her husband set her at the center of their bed and made short work of his clothing — although his nice cobalt button-down was done for, if the pinging buttons were any indication.

"Jared, that shirt was expensive!" She laughed through her complaint.

"Don't care," he answered as he shrugged out of it, yanked his zipper down and shoved his dark jeans off his hips. He tossed his cowboy boots across the room one-by-one, and prowled to their king-sized bed.

She giggled. "No undies? How did I not notice that?" Her gaze zoned in on his erection and she licked her lips.

Jared groaned. "It was a bad call."

"Why?"

"Chafing. If the blue balls weren't enough."

Mel laughed yet again.

He flashed a grin when their gazes brushed.

Her insides wobbled. Her husband was *hot*.

"It's your fault, really," she said.

"Mine? How'd you figure? You made me want you."

Heat flushed her body and she quivered. Burned for his hands on her. She raised her arms in invitation, and he didn't disappoint.

Jared practically pounced on the bed and hovered over her.

She dragged her fingers down his chest, traced his abs and watched his muscles jump under her touch.

When Mel looked into his face, her husband had his head back, eyes closed, a look of desire and contentment dominating his expression.

Her insides shook all over. *She* had the power to make him look like that.

"Jared," she whispered.

His gorgeous dark eyes met hers. "Hmm, baby?"

"Baby. Exactly. Let's make one."

He grinned, but then sobered. Cupped her face. "I love you, and I want you, but it *will* be okay if it doesn't happen this time."

She smiled. "I love you, too. And I always want you."

"Mel."

Her name was all warning.

"Relax, I'm in a good place. Promise."

Jared studied her for a few more seconds before his big shoulders loosened. "I was there, too."

"What?"

"Doc Hayes says we're good. My swimmers swim, and he said it can take up to a year."

Mel smiled. She really was better with things after her appointment last week. She needed him to believe she wasn't a head-case.

Despair had melted in to reserved hopefulness.

There was nothing *wrong* with either of them.

"I know, love. I'm okay, really. I just want to feel good with you. That's my mindset now. I'm not obsessing about what the monitor told me. I mean, I'm aware it's there, but it's in the back of my mind."

He narrowed his eyes. "You sure?"

"Hey, if I can think, you're not doing something right. Isn't that what you always say?"

"I *always* do it right," Jared growled and kissed her.

It was a quick thing that was over much too soon.

She giggled and patted his cheek. "Time to prove it again, husband."

Chapter Seven

JARED HELD HIMSELF over his naked wife. His gorgeous, flushed pink with desire, ravished-looking wife, and he was only getting started.

She didn't need to challenge him, because he was *so* already there. Had been all day.

He *did* want to make sure she was okay—really okay. She *had* seemed more lighthearted about the baby thing since the appointment last week.

"You sure?" he quizzed her once more.

Not that she'd lie, but she would minimize so he wouldn't worry.

That was classic Mel.

She frowned, but her mouth wobbled with the smile she was fighting—she wasn't really irritated. "You're gonna let me doubt you like that and get away with it?"

He smirked. "Doubt me? Puhllleassse. We both know *my* skills, baby." He punctuated his response with the tilt of his pelvis, and rubbed his cock against her sex.

She moaned and closed her eyes. Lifted her torso, drawing his attention to her peaked dusky nipples.

Jared skimmed his palms over her breasts and she pressed into his hands. He groaned, and his balls ached. "Now that's what I'm talkin' about."

Mel pinned him with those crystal eyes. "Done. Talking. Show. Time." She lifted her hips and shoved against him, ripping another groan from *his* lips.

He had to pant to get air down. He grabbed his dick and ran his tip up and down her glistening tender flesh, then parted her folds and circled her clit, pushing their skin together.

"Jared…" she whispered, elongating his name on a pleasurable sigh.

He smiled and stopped the torture, propelling inside her.

They both moaned.

"You win," he grunted with his first thrust.

"We both win," Mel whimpered, and slid her arms around his neck. She urged him down for a kiss, and he didn't resist.

He took her mouth, tasting the wine she'd had with dinner and something sweet that was just his wife. Something familiar and lovely that made him sear even hotter for her, until his temples pounded with his rushing pulse, and he timed his surges forward in rhythm; his tongue and his hips.

Jared had wanted to worship her, but he'd been too revved up all day. This wouldn't last long enough. He'd make it up to her, because he was far from done with her.

Not that she looked bothered when he ended their latest kiss to take a breath.

Her eyes were closed and she clung to him as he drove forward even harder; just how she liked it.

Mel's hands slid down his damp back, landing a tight grip on his ass, where she kneaded and squeezed. She lifted her bottom, moving with him, against him, holding him even tighter.

He bit his bottom lip as his spine and his balls tingled. Damn, he was close, too quick indeed. He'd owe her one — or three.

Her sex quivered and she whimpered.

His wife was close, too.

Good.

At least she'd come, too. Jared wouldn't have it any other way.

He pulled back only to jolt forward on a grunt, and her nails dug into his biceps. He didn't give a shit. The smart there only made his pleasure below even sharper.

Mel screeched some representation of his name, but it faded with the tilt of her chin as she threw her head back and the glorious waves of her light brown tresses flew up.

When she screamed, it didn't have to be anything intelligible. When her eyes went hazy and couldn't focus, when she exposed her neck and lifted her perfect breasts into his chest. When her hair was even more mussed than his hands could make it.

When she melded into him and held so tightly he couldn't breathe.

That was when he loved her best.

It didn't matter where his touch was on her body. It didn't matter if he was inside her. It only mattered that *he* was the cause of that particular look on her face.

Loss of control. Utter desperation for release.

For *him*.

Then she would grasp at him and whisper his name.

Every. Damn. Time.

Jared was in his glory at those moments. And not just because he was getting laid.

She was his.

He was hers.

The love of his life. In his arms. In his bed.

For the rest of his life.

His orgasm exploded inside her at the same time Mel's sex contracted and released around him. He hissed at the intensity as her body milked his.

Jared pinned her to his chest and took her mouth.

She was right there with him, kissing him hard. Their lips and tongues wrestled, mixed in with teeth, nibbles and nips as they both panted for air.

"Jared," Mel whimpered into his mouth.

His muscles ached, begging him to loosen, so he obeyed, slipping from her center and rolling to his back. The cool sheets shocked his shoulder blades, but the contrast to his overheated form felt good.

He tugged his wife into his arms and pressed a kiss to her forehead, brushing her damp hair from where it clung.

"Love you," she breathed, her warm breath tickling his neck.

"I love you, too, baby." He smiled at the heavy-lidded quality that still remained over her beautiful eyes. He cupped her cheek and ran his thumb over her flushed skin. "Next time, I'm going to taste you." Jared dragged his free hand down her stomach and skimmed his fingers between her legs.

She shivered and snuggled closer.

He laughed when she didn't speak. "Damn, I'm good."

Mel lifted her head from his chest and flashed a sexy smirk. "Wow."

"Yeah, you could say that, too."

His wife rolled her eyes.

He grinned.

"Just in time, I guess," she said.

"For what?"

"You can check your ego at the door when you do your chores."

"Chores?"

Mel patted his right pec. "You have to go finish the kitchen."

Jared gasped. "Whhhhat? After I rocked your world? I don't get a pass?"

She mock-glared. "I thought your wife wasn't to be trifled with?"

He shook his head and chuckled, then tried to school his expression, but it was hard to hide a smile. "It's not nice to throw one's words back in their face."

She giggled. "You can't even say that with a straight face."

"Oh, all right. But I'm taking payment afterward."

"Payment? I cooked all day, the least you can do is clean up!"

He grinned again. "So? Payment is still necessary."

"What?" Her expression was mock-outraged.

Jared kissed her until she moaned into his lips and his cock jumped—despite just having been wrung out.

Mel's arms shot around his neck, and she squeezed him against her.

He laughed again. "Seems like you'll like the payment just fine."

"You said you were going to taste me next time."

It was his turn to shiver as the words danced over his shoulders and down his spine, then made his dick jolt again.

Damn, when she said stuff like that—

He groaned and kissed her again, but she smacked his ass with a loud *sound* that smarted.

"Hey!" Jared rubbed his throbbing right cheek.

Her grin was mischievous when their eyes met.

"Clean up, then I'd be happy to let you have *payment.* Since there's something in it for me, of course." Mel winked and he couldn't help but laugh again.

"You should kiss my boo boo, first." He bit his bottom lip to keep from grinning and pointed to his ass cheek.

His wife arched an eyebrow. "I'll smack it again, *first.*" She lifted her hand.

Jared scrambled off the bed. "Okay, okay. I'll go." He threw his palms up.

"I'll be waiting for you."

"Stay. Naked." He waggled his eyebrows.

She giggled. "Yes, sir."

He made a show of looking her up and down and smiled softly at her pink cheeks and how she fidgeted.

His wife was so hot; a mix of innocence and vixen.

He wanted to ignore her orders and get back in bed. Was almost ready to take her again.

"Hey, pick up my clothes, too."

Jared pointed. "Hey, don't push it." He left the bedroom, grinning when she giggled.

Chapter Eight

THE LITTLE BLUE plus sign blurred, but her eyes were at fault; nothing was wrong with the early pregnancy test on the bathroom counter.

Mel sniffled and wiped her face.

Her heart and stomach jumped at the same time, and she blinked a few times, to make sure she wasn't hallucinating.

It wasn't wishful thinking this time.

The test was positive.

I'm pregnant.

She and Jared were going to have a baby.

Mel plastered her hand to her lower belly.

I'm going to be a mother.

More tears were born and spilled, hot on her cheeks.

"Mel, I'm gonna head out. Cole called." Her husband popped his head into the bathroom, then froze in the doorframe. "Why the hell are you crying?" Jared's handsome face was suddenly all angry lines; he looked like he wanted to kill something—or someone—for upsetting her.

She smiled through her tears. Loved him even more for his instant need to slay all her dragons.

He was at her side in seconds, taking her hand in his and bringing her knuckles to his mouth. He planted a kiss there, then cupped her face and thumbed her cheeks dry. "Baby?" he whispered.

"Look." She lifted the test from the edge of the sink.

Jared's gorgeous dark eyes widened — then went misty.

Mel's heart stuttered all over again.

He's crying, too?

She bit her lip to stifle a sob, and launched herself at him.

Her husband caught her up and held her close. Rubbed her back in slow, soothing circles.

Minutes that felt like wonderful hours passed, and Mel squeezed her eyes shut against his shoulder and nestled closer.

"Really?" he whispered when he leaned back, his big hands landing on her upper arms.

Jared's expression held love and wonder that made her insides wobble.

She was grateful he'd been so strong every month she'd started her period. Every month she wasn't pregnant.

This was the expression she'd craved — proof he wanted this as much as she did. She would've been crushed to see the disappointment on his face that *she'd* felt at each failure.

He'd meant it when he'd reassured her.

It would happen when it was supposed to.

And it finally *had*.

She smiled through more tears and nodded. "Baby."

"Baby," Jared echoed.

Whether his normal endearment for her, or a reference to what grew inside her, it didn't make Mel's hands shake any less when she cupped his cheeks. She nodded again, because words *so* weren't happening at the moment.

"I love you," he breathed.

"I love you, too," she finally managed.

Silence fell, but then they made eye contact, they exchanged a smile.

"Guess what," Jared whispered.

"What?"

"Thanksgiving is my new favorite holiday." He put his hand over her lower tummy.

Mel grinned and rested her palm over his. "In that case, I won't tell my dad how you really feel about him."

Surprise lit his dark eyes, then her husband threw his head back and laughed.

The End

About the Author

USA TODAY Bestselling, award winning author of historical and epic fantasy romance, as well as romantic suspense, C.A. loves to dabble in different genres. If it's a good story, she'll write it, no matter where it seems to fit! She's a hopeless romantic and always will be.

Risking it all for Happily Ever After is what she lives by!

C.A. is originally from Ohio, but got to Texas as soon as she could. She's happily married and has a bachelor's degree in Criminal Justice.

She works with kids when she's not writing.

WEBSITE: http://www.caszarek.com
BLOG: http://www.caszarekwriter.blogspot.com/
TWITTER: https://twitter.com/caszarek
FACEBOOK: http://www.facebook.com/caszarek
INSTAGRAM: https://www.instagram.com/caszarek/
GOODREADS:https://www.goodreads.com/author/show/5815085.C_A_Szarek
NEWSLETTER SIGNUP: http://blogspot.us7.list-manage.com/subscribe?u=296abc5983ebc51c1d4d0972b&id=fb22ce93be
EMAIL: ca@caszarek.com